BEECHWOOD BUNNY TALES

PERIWINKLE
at the
Full Moon Ball

For a free color catalog describing Gareth Stevens' list of high-quality children's books, call 1-800-341-3569 (USA) or 1-800-461-9120 (Canada).

Beechwood Bunny Tales
Dandelion's Vanishing Vegetable Garden
Mistletoe and the Baobab Tree
Periwinkle at the Full Moon Ball
Poppy's Dance

Library of Congress Cataloging-in-Publication Data

Huriet, Geneviève.
  [Premier bal d'Agaric Passiflore. English]
  Periwinkle at the full moon ball / illustrated by Loïc Jouannigot ; written by Geneviève
Huriet. — North American ed.
     p. cm. — (Beechwood bunny tales)
  Translation of: Le premier bal d'Agaric Passiflore.
  Summary: Afraid that he'll embarrass the more graceful members of his family at
the Full Moon Ball, Periwinkle the rabbit accepts dancing lessons from a tricky magpie.
  ISBN 0-8368-0525-9
  [1. Dancing—Fiction. 2. Rabbits—Fiction. 3. Animals—Fiction.] I. Jouannigot,
Loïc, ill. II. Title. III. Series.
PZ7.H95657Pe   1991   [E]—dc20   90-46859

North American edition first published in 1991 by
Gareth Stevens Children's Books
1555 North RiverCenter Drive, Suite 201
Milwaukee, Wisconsin 53212, USA

English text by MaryLee Knowlton

Printed in the United States of America

1 2 3 4 5 6 7 8 9 95 94 93 92 91

BEECHWOOD BUNNY TALES

PERIWINKLE
at the
Full Moon Ball

written by GENEVIÈVE HURIET   illustrated by LOÏC JOUANNIGOT

Gareth Stevens Children's Books
MILWAUKEE

The bunnies of Beechwood Grove love to dance. Light a meadow with a moonbeam, and they will dance till dawn.

The Beechwood Grove Full Moon Ball was the best dance of the year. All of the Bellflower bunnies would be there this year.

Mistletoe and Dandelion giggled at the thought of it. But not Periwinkle.

"I don't know how to dance," he said with a frown.

"Don't worry about it, dear," said Aunt Zinnia gently. "As everyone knows, all bunnies can dance."

"Especially Bellflower bunnies," Papa Bramble added proudly. "We have always been fine dancers."

Violette tried to cheer Periwinkle.
"You'll have a wonderful time," she said.
"Just watch us and do what we do."
But Periwinkle was not convinced.

"What if it doesn't come to me?" he wondered sadly. "What if the steps are not in my feet?"

Periwinkle became more and more certain: he was not a dancing bunny.

Periwinkle sighed a deep sigh, imagining how he would disgrace the whole Bellflower family.

"What's the matter, little bunny?" he heard a voice ask. It was Magda the magpie: thief, busybody, and trickster.

"Tell Magda everything," she urged, pretending to be sweet. Little Periwinkle poured out his troubles to her.

Magda grinned sneakily as she took the troubled bunny under her wing. "Dance lessons are what you need," she said. "Just leave everything to Magda."

The next morning, Magda and Periwinkle met in the woods. "Your first teacher will be the wood pigeon," said Magda. "He has the prettiest strut."

"Watch carefully," the pigeon said. "Three steps right, and bow. Three steps left, and bow. Now you try it."

Periwinkle began stepping and bowing smartly. All day long, teacher and student strutted. "Tippee, tippee, tip, bow. Tappee, tappee, tap, bow. Fluff out your feathers, . . . I mean . . . your fur. Begin again! Tippee, tippee . . ."

12

Finally the pigeon was satisfied. "You're a fine dancer, Periwinkle." Hidden nearby, crafty old Magda cackled gleefully. Everything was shaping up just as she had planned.

Periwinkle arrived home stiff and very hungry that night.

"Where have you been all day, Peri?" asked Aunt Zinnia.

"Oh, in the woods . . . with friends," replied Periwinkle, and he quickly ate dinner and went to bed before anyone could ask more questions.

The next morning, Periwinkle and Magda met again. "Today we're going to see Rainette the frog," Magda told Periwinkle. "She has the best leaping legs in the business."

And with her fast-talking ways, Magda persuaded Rainette to teach the bunny to jump.

"Pay attention, bunny," Rainette grumped. "It's all in the back legs. These are the basic jumps: poing, poing, hop, and into the grass. Finally, the most glorious of all: poing, poing, plouf, and into the pond!"

"Oh, no!" begged Periwinkle. "Ponds are not good for bunnies!"

"As you wish. Begin!" sniffed
Rainette. And all day, Periwinkle
poinged and ploufed, ploufed
and poinged.

"Head up! Back straight!
Breathe in time! Higher!
Higher!" Rainette was a stern
teacher. But by the end of the
lesson, Periwinkle could poing
and plouf with the best of them.

At home, the Bellflower bunnies thought of nothing but the Full Moon Ball. Violette swayed as she tried on dress after dress. Dandelion tapped his feet, buttoning his new vest. Mistletoe tried a new hairstyle every night. He hummed as he parted it first one way and then another. Even studious Poppy sashayed slightly as he read.

And all the while, Periwinkle just continued to practice his jumps and struts.

"How do you do that?" Poppy demanded. "You jump even farther than I do, and I'm the biggest!"

"It's all in the back legs," was all Periwinkle would answer.

At last came the night of the Full Moon Ball. The Bellflower bunnies made a splendid entrance just as the owl began the festivities.

Perched in a nearby tree, Magda leaned forward eagerly. She wanted to watch Periwinkle embarrass himself by strutting like a pigeon and hopping like a frog. As the moon rose, the dancing began. Aunt Zinnia moved slowly with tiny, proper steps. Papa danced seriously, slightly off beat.

The younger Bellflower bunnies joined their friends in a frenzy of jumping, tapping, wiggling, and turning.

Periwinkle, confident after his dance lessons, plunged right in, strutting and jumping. Tippee, tippee, tip, bow! Poing, poing! The other bunnies noticed his strange movements and stopped dancing to watch. Before long, Periwinkle was the only one dancing.

In the shadows, Magda laughed nastily. The bunnies began to titter and giggle. Periwinkle's cheeks began to burn, and his stomach felt queasy. What was happening here?

In a moment, the wise old owl understood what was going on. A glance at Magda and another at Periwinkle told her all she needed to know. Magda wanted all the bunnies of Beechwood Grove to laugh at little Periwinkle.

The owl spread her wings and glided to the ground. "My friends," she said gravely, "tonight we are honored to have a very talented bunny among us — Periwinkle Bellflower. Who can name the animals he has been imitating?"

The laughter stopped. At the owl's request, Periwinkle repeated his first dance. Tippee, tippee, tip, bow. Tappee, tappee, tap, bow.

A tiny voice called out, "It's the wood pigeon!" The forest echoed with applause.

Then Periwinkle did his jumps. Poing, poing, plouf! Poing, poing, plouf! Everyone cheered: "Bravo! Bravo! It's the frog!"

As Periwinkle took his final bows, the bunnies began to dance again.

And then the strangest thing happened. In the company of his family and friends, Periwinkle forgot all about his dance lessons. For the rest of the long summer night, he danced like all the other bunnies.

At dawn, the Bellflower bunnies and their friends headed home. Leading the line was Periwinkle, tired but happy and proud.

And Magda? What about Magda? Well, tricked by her own trick, she slunk home to bed.

And no one missed her one bit.